TO BABY

from Daddy

A LOVE LETTER FROM A FATHER TO A DAUGHTER

Written and illustrated by
STEVE NGUYEN

Sky Pony Press
New York, NY

Visit our website at www.skyponypress.com.

10 9 8 7 6 5 4 3 2 1

Manufactured in China, February 2020
This product conforms to CPSIA 2008

Library of Congress Cataloging-in-Publication Data is available on file.

Jacket artwork and design by Steve Nguyen

Print ISBN: 978-1-5107-4599-5
Ebook ISBN: 978-1-5107-4600-8

To Priscilla, Stella, and all the daddies about to embark on this wonderful journey of fatherhood.

S.N.

To

_____

From

_____

To Baby

It is very important for you to know . . .
there are many things to learn as you grow.

Look up above, way up high . . .

and there, you will see the great night sky.

If you look above and far . . .
you will see your
destiny in the stars.

The stars are a reminder that you are a blessing . . .
and that your story is always progressing.

Your mommy's love for you will never fade . . .

and there's nothing in the world that she would trade.

I encourage you to travel to
different places.

Try new things and see new faces.

The beach is my favorite place to play . . .
because I have taken you there every day.

In your life, you will encounter various creatures.

Take the time to admire their unique features.

All the creatures in this wonderful place,
show just how much beauty surrounds
this space.

When you are lost, look to
that star way up high . . .

Build meaningful bridges
with those you adore.

Those are what special friendships are for.

The seeds we plant in the ground,
grow into beautiful plants and flowers
all around.

As the wind's whistles make their rounds,
close your eyes and listen to the sounds.

The beautiful music in the air . . .
is a gift from nature that we all
can share.

I will always be there to guide you through
the journeys you will soon pursue.

The last thing I want to share with you is love . . .
because you were created from the heavens above.

Kindness and love are hard to spare . . .
but the most important thing is for you to care.

When you are older, come with me . . .
where I've buried a box
beside the old tree.

Inside this box, you will find . . .
all the memories I have kept over time.

The message I have kept in this jar . . .
is a reminder that daddy will always love you,
my bright and shining star.

I would like to thank all of the folks at Skyhorse Publishing and Sky Pony Press, especially my editor Jason Katzman, who advocated for my book and worked so hard to make this dream a reality. I would also like to thank my fellow artist and longtime friend Alex Solis, who helped me realize my potential as an artist and offered advice and support when I needed it the most, and Cole Adams for taking his time to help with the edits. Special thanks to Marala Scott for her inspirational literary work and for always believing in me. My gratitude extends to my beloved Studio APA crew, Choz Belen and Tsan Tsai. Your ability to create captivating visuals have inspired and pushed me tremendously throughout this process.

I want to thank my wife Priscilla, my parents Benjamin and Denise, my brother Ryan, and my sister Kristine for being incredibly supportive of my endeavors during the making of this book. Last but not least, my daughter, Stella Gee Nguyen, for making this all possible.

—S.N.